·

Britain has entered the twentieth century. Queen Victoria is dead and the Boer War rages on. Inspector Lestrade is called upon to investigate the brutal death of Ralph Childers, MP. It is but the first in a series of bizarre and perplexing murders that lead Lestrade around the country in the pursuit of his enquiries.

The connection between the victims appears to be politics. Is someone trying to destroy the Government? It would seem so, particularly when a bomb is found in the Palace of Westminster. But who is responsible? The Fenians? Or have the Suffragettes decided upon a more drastic course of action to further their cause?

During his investigations Lestrade encounters some old and some new faces. Amongst the new ones are the brother and cousin of the late Sherlock Holmes who died eleven years ago at the Reichenbach Falls. But is Holmes really dead? Dr Watson doesn't think so. Someone wants to keep Holmes alive and Lestrade is forced to 'tread the boards' (playing himself) to discover the truth. And, as if things aren't serious enough, the King is kidnapped just before his coronation.

Amidst all this Lestrade is faced with the knowledge that his daughter is growing up not knowing who her real father is.

Full of the wry humour and gentle appreciation of the era that were apparent in *The Adventures of Inspector Lestrade* and *Brigade*, M J Trow brings us another entrancing and puzzling episode in the career of Inspector Sholto Lestrade.

THE ADVENTURES OF INSPECTOR LESTRADE
BRIGADE